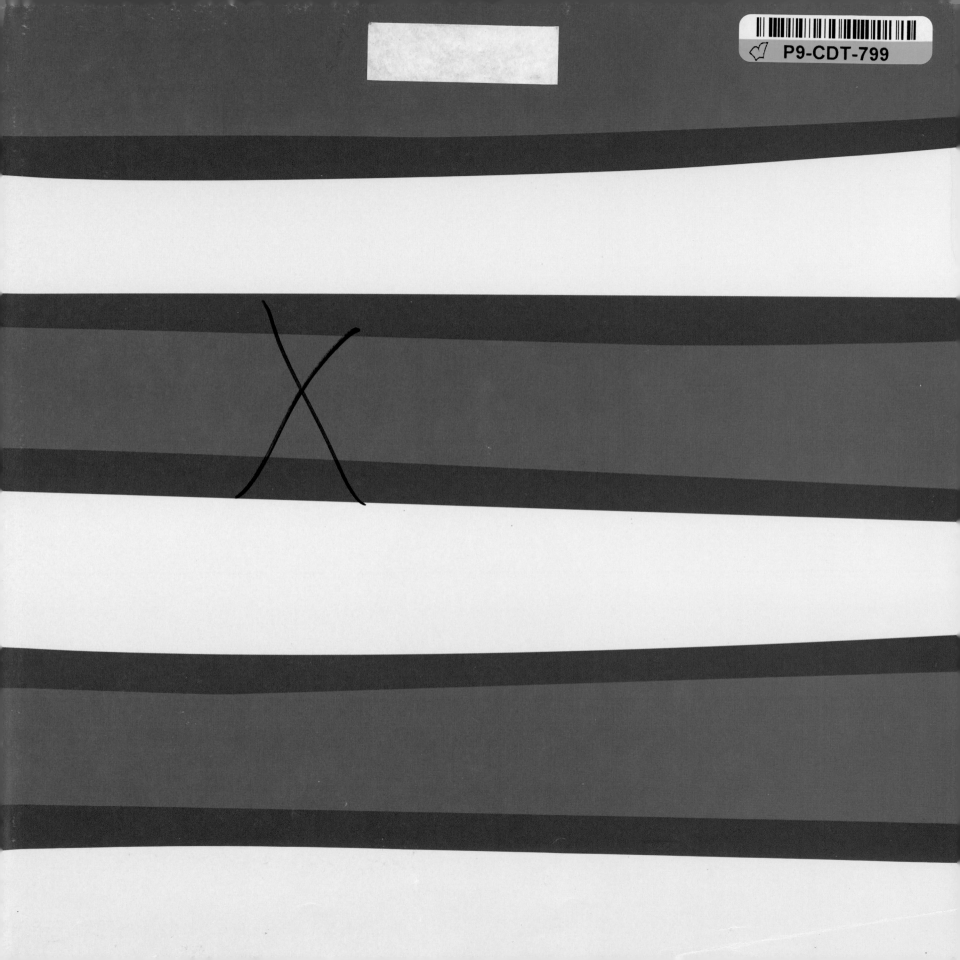

WHY DID THE CHICKEN CROSS THE ROAD?

IN PECKING ORDER:

MARLA FRAZEE

MO WILLEMS

JUDY SCHACHNER

TEDD ARNOLD

DAVID SHANNON

JON AGEE

VLADIMIR RADUNSKY

JERRY PINKNEY

CHRIS SHEBAN

HARRY BLISS

MARY GRANDPRÉ

LYNN MUNSINGER

DAVID CATROW

CHRIS RASCHKA

**DIAL BOOKS
FOR YOUNG READERS**

DIAL BOOKS FOR YOUNG READERS ·
A division of Penguin Young Readers
Group · Published by The Penguin Group ·
Penguin Group (USA) Inc., 375 Hudson Street,
New York, NY 10014, U.S.A. · Penguin Group
(Canada), 90 Eglinton Avenue East, Suite 700,
Toronto, Ontario, Canada M4P 2Y3 (a division of
Pearson Penguin Canada Inc.) · Penguin Books Ltd, 80
Strand, London WC2R 0RL, England · Penguin Ireland, 25
St. Stephen's Green, Dublin 2, Ireland (a division of Penguin
Books Ltd) · Penguin Books India Pvt Ltd, 11 Community Centre,
Panchsheel Park, New Delhi - 110 017, India · Penguin Group (NZ),
Cnr Airborne and Rosedale Roads, Albany, Auckland, New Zealand
(a division of Pearson New Zealand Ltd) · Penguin Books (South Africa)
(Pty) Ltd, 24 Sturdee Avenue, Rosebank, Johannesburg 2196, South Africa ·
Penguin Books Ltd, Registered Offices: 80 Strand, London WC2R 0RL, England

Pages:
8–9 copyright © 2006 by Marla Frazee;
10–11 copyright © 2006 by Mo Willems;
12–13 copyright © 2006 by Judith Byron Schachner;
14–15 copyright © 2006 by Tedd Arnold;
16–17 copyright © 2006 by David Shannon;
18–19 copyright © 2006 by Jon Agee;
20–21 copyright © 2006 by Vladimir Radunsky;
22–23 copyright © 2006 by Jerry Pinkney;
24–25 copyright © 2006 by Chris Sheban;
26–27 copyright © 2006 by Harry Bliss;
28–29 copyright © 2006 by Mary GrandPré;
30–31 copyright © 2006 by Lynn Munsinger;
32–33 copyright © 2006 by David Catrow;
34–35 copyright © 2006 by Chris Raschka
All rights reserved
Designed by Teresa Kietlinski Dikun

Library of Congress Cataloging-in-Publication Data
Why did the chicken cross the road? / Jon Agee . . . [et al.].
    p. cm.   ISBN 0-8037-3203-1
1. Chickens—Caricatures and cartoons—Juvenile
literature. 2. American wit and humor, Pictorial—
Juvenile literature. I. Agee, Jon.
NC1763.C43W49 2006
741.5'973—dc22   2005016196

1 3 5 7 9 10 8 6 4 2
Manufactured in China on acid-free paper

WHY DID the CHICKEN CROSS the ROAD?

art by MARLA FRAZEE

she was de-ranged!

art by TEDD ARNOLD

Because the
light was green!

art by DAVID SHANNON

art by JON AGEE

Why did the chicken cross the road?

art by VLADIMIR RADUNSKY

Because his sister's marrying Toad.

art by
JERRY PINKNEY

art by CHRIS SHEBAN

Ask the mutated zombie chickens from Mars!

art by MARY GRANDPRÉ

art by LYNN MUNSINGER

Why did the chicken cross the road?
Because the light said "walk."

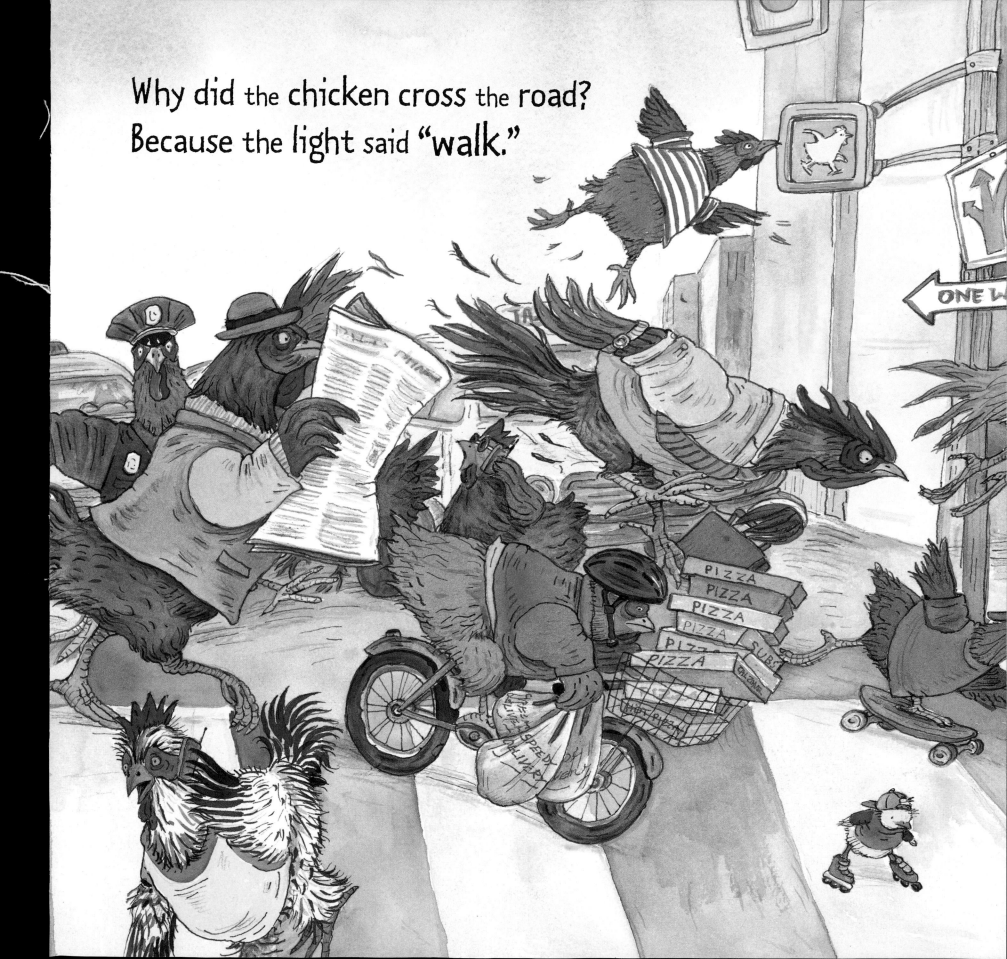

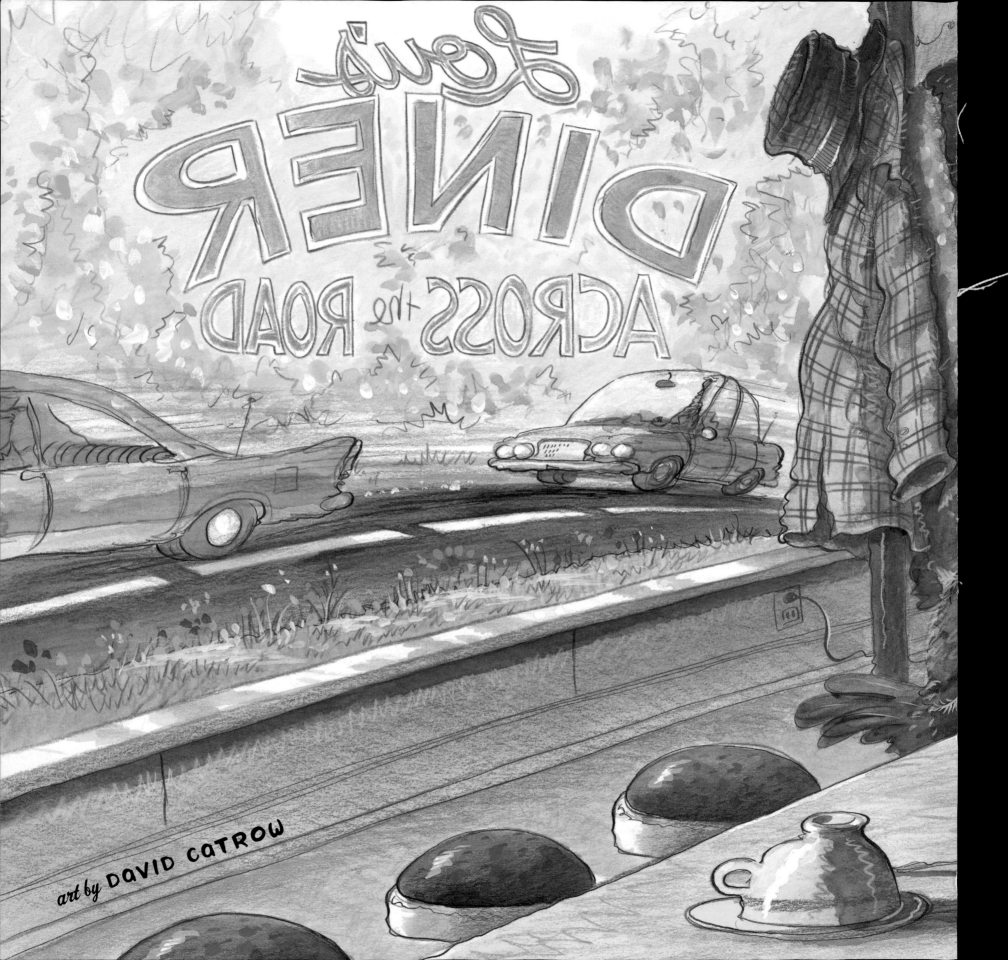

JON AGEE CROSSED
to finish his portrait of the chicken.

JON AGEE'S BOOKS INCLUDE:
Terrific;
Milo's Hat Trick;
Z Goes Home

HARRY BLISS CROSSED
to paint the **other side.**

HARRY BLISS'S BOOKS INCLUDE:
Diary of a Spider and *Diary of a Worm*, by Doreen Cronin; *A Fine, Fine School*, by Sharon Creech

TEDD ARNOLD SAID:
"Well, see, I was in the middle of making a cool drawing of this chicken when it up and crossed the road. I had to finish my drawing, so I followed it. So you better **ask the chicken why it crossed . . .**
Oh, never mind."

TEDD ARNOLD'S BOOKS INCLUDE:
Parts; *Axle Annie and the Speed Grump*, by Robin Pulver; *No Jumping on the Bed!*

CHRIS RASCHKA CROSSED
because **he didn't own a car.**

CHRIS RASCHKA'S BOOKS INCLUDE:
John Coltrane's Giant Steps; *The Hello, Goodbye Window*, by Norton Juster; *A Poke in the I*, by Paul Janeczko

MARLA FRAZEE CROSSED to put it all in perspective.

MARLA FRAZEE'S BOOKS INCLUDE: *Roller Coaster*; *Santa Claus the World's Number One Toy Expert*; *Walk On! A Guide for Babies of All Ages*

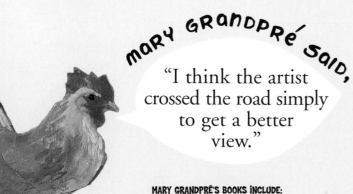

MARY GRANDPRÉ SAID,
"I think the artist crossed the road simply to get a better view."

MARY GRANDPRÉ'S BOOKS INCLUDE:
Henry and Pawl and the Round Yellow Ball, co-authored with Tom Casmer; *The Sea Chest*, by Toni Buzzeo; the Harry Potter series

DAVID CATROW CROSSED
because he thinks he might have left his glasses there.

DAVID CATROW'S BOOKS INCLUDE:
Wet Dog!, by Elise Broach; *Stand Tall, Molly Lou Melon*, by Patty Lovell; *We the Kids*

LYNN MUNSINGER SAID,
"At first I was afraid I might fowl up, but then I decided I better not **chicken** out."

CHRIS SHEBAN CROSSED to go to law school (like the chicken).

CHRIS SHEBAN'S BOOKS INCLUDE:
I Met a Dinosaur, by Jan Wahl; *The Shoe Tree of Chagrin*, by J. Patrick Lewis; *The Story of a Seagull and the Cat Who Taught Her to Fly*, by Luis Sepúlveda

MO WILLEMS CROSSED
to avoid answering **this** question!

LYNN MUNSINGER'S BOOKS INCLUDE:
What Mommies Do Best / What Daddies Do Best, by Laura Numeroff; *Tacky and the Winter Games*, by Helen Lester; *Seven Spunky Monkeys*, by Jackie French Koller

JUDY SCHACHNER CROSSED
because she is one **crazy** chick who loves to **fox-trot** over every skyway, highway, byway, lane, shunpike, interstate, and street that comes her way. "Hallelujah, hens, let's dance!"

JUDY SCHACHNER'S BOOKS INCLUDE:
Skippyjon Jones and *Skippyjon Jones in the Doghouse*; *Yo, Vikings!*; *I Know an Old Lady Who Swallowed a Pie*, by Alison Jackson

MO WILLEMS'S BOOKS INCLUDE:
Don't Let the Pigeon Drive the Bus!; *Knuffle Bunny: A Cautionary Tale*; *Leonardo, the Terrible Monster*

VLADIMIR RADUNSKY REPLIED.
"Curiosity,"

VLADIMIR RADUNSKY'S BOOKS INCLUDE:
The Maestro Plays, by Bill Martin Jr.; *The Mighty Asparagus*; *Ten*; *One*

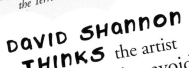

DAVID SHANNON THINKS the artist crossed the road to avoid his landlord, whom he owed rent. Or maybe it was because he thought the grass was greener. Or he wanted to keep on the sunny side. I don't know, you never can tell with those artist types.

DAVID SHANNON'S BOOKS INCLUDE:
No, David!; *How I Became a Pirate*, by Melinda Long; *Alice the Fairy*

JERRY PINKNEY SAID,
"Why did the **chicken** cross the road? In **my** search for an answer to this age-old riddle, I queried friends, librarians, teachers, and a car service driver. Most of them responded with 'Oh, that's an easy one . . . to get to the other side!' I was uninspired with the same reply over and over again. So I crossed the road, found the Little Red Hen, and asked her."

JERRY PINKNEY'S BOOKS INCLUDE:
The Little Red Hen; *The Old African*, by Julius Lester; *The Ugly Duckling*

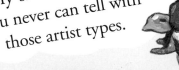